P9-DHT-646

CREVE COEUR PUBLIC LIBRARY DIST.

A35520 426406

DATE DUE

AUG 1 1 10	MAY 1 4 15
OCT 7 10	
NOV 05 10	
SEP 30 11	
OCT 27 11	
NOV 03 11	
DEC 01 11	
FEB 9 12	
MAR 1 5 12	
MAR 29 12	
MAY 3 12	
MAY 1 0 12	
OCT 0 9 2013	

Word After
Word After Word

ALSO BY
PATRICIA MacLACHLAN

All the Places to Love

What You Know First

Three Names

Who Loves Me?

WRITTEN WITH
EMILY MacLACHLAN CHAREST

Painting the Wind

Bittle

Once I Ate a Pie

Fiona Loves the Night

PATRICIA MacLACHLAN

Word After
Word After Word

KATHERINE TEGEN BOOKS
An Imprint of HarperCollinsPublishers

Excerpt on page 32 from *Charlotte's Web* by E.B. White. Copyright 1952 by E.B. White. Text copyright renewed 1980 by E.B. White. Used by permission of HarperCollins Publishers. Excerpt on pages 32–33 from *Tuck Everlasting* by Natalie Babbitt. Copyright © 1975, renewed 2003 by Natalie Babbitt. Reprinted by permission of Farrar, Straus and Giroux, LLC. Excerpt on pages 33–34 from *Sarah, Plain and Tall* by Patricia MacLachlan. Copyright © 1985 by Patricia MacLachlan. Used by permission of HarperCollins Publishers. Excerpt on page 35 from *Baby* by Patricia MacLachlan. Used by permission of Random House, Inc.

Katherine Tegen Books
is an imprint of HarperCollins Publishers.

Word After Word After Word
Copyright © 2010 by Patricia MacLachlan
All rights reserved.
Printed in the United States of America.
No part of this book may be used or reproduced in any manner whatsoever without written permission except in the case of brief quotations embodied in critical articles and reviews. For information address HarperCollins Children's Books, a division of HarperCollins Publishers, 10 East 53rd Street, New York, NY 10022.
www.harpercollinschildrens.com

Library of Congress Cataloging-in-Publication Data
MacLachlan, Patricia.
Word after word after word / Patricia MacLachlan. — 1st ed.
p. cm.
Summary: A visiting author teaches five friends about the power of words and writing.
ISBN 978-0-06-027971-4 (trade bdg.) — ISBN 978-0-06-027972-1 (lib. bdg.)
[1. Writing—Fiction. 2. Authorship—Fiction. 3. Schools—Fiction.] I. Title.
PZ7.M2225Wo 2010   2009026708
[Fic]—dc22   CIP
                                                                 AC

10 11 12 13 14   CG/RRDB   10 9 8 7 6 5 4 3 2 1
❖
First Edition

For Craig Virden.
With love,
P.M.

Contents

I write entirely to find out what I'm thinking, what I'm looking at, what I see and what it means. What I want and what I fear.

—Joan Didion

Chapter 1

Some things happen in fours.
On the fourth day of the fourth
month after the winter holiday vacation,
a famous writer came to our fourth-
grade class. Her name was Ms. Mirabel.
She liked the "Ms." a lot. She hissed

"Ms." like Evie's cat, Looley, hissed. I looked over at Evie and she was smiling. She had thought of Looley, too.

Ms. Mirabel had long, troubled hair and a chest that pushed out in front of her like a grocery cart.

"Did you always want to be a writer?" asked Henry.

He smiled at me. Hen carried a notebook with him at all times, sometimes stopping in the middle of soccer practice to pull it out and write something.

"No," said Ms. Mirabel. "I wanted to be a stage performer or an electrical engineer."

"How much money do you make?" asked Evie.

"Evie," warned our teacher, Miss Cash. "That's not a proper question to ask."

"That's all right," said Ms. Mirabel cheerfully. "I make enough to send my children to camp in the summer."

Evie frowned. She hated camp. She had once said that only cruel and uninterested parents sent their children off to camp in the summer. Evie knew firsthand. Her parents had sent her off to Camp Minnetuba the summer that they separated. When Evie returned home, her mother had moved out; her father lived there with Evie and her little brother, Thomas.

"Temporary," said her father and mother. "It has nothing to do with you."

Evie thought it had lots to do with her. From time to time her mother visited, but she never stayed very long.

"Is what you write real?" asked May.

Ms. Mirabel brightened. She liked that question.

"Real or unreal. They're just about the same," said Ms. Mirabel. "They are both all about magical words!"

She said *words* with a soft hush in her voice.

"Do you write with an outline?" Russell asked.

Ms. Mirabel laughed loudly. It was a sudden, startling laugh; and we all laughed, too.

"Of course not," she said. "Outlines are silly. Once you write the outline, there's no reason to write the story. You write to participate . . . to find out what is going to happen!"

Miss Cash frowned. This is not what she had taught us in creative writing class.

"Actually, I loathe outlines!" said Ms. Mirabel with great feeling.

Miss Cash closed her eyes as if her head hurt.

And then Hen asked the question that made all the difference to us.

"Why do you write?" he asked.

Ms. Mirabel sighed. There was a sudden hush in the room, as if Ms. Mirabel was about to say something very important.

As it turned out, she was.

"I, myself, write to change my life, to make it come out the way I want it to," she said. "But other people write for other reasons: to see more closely what it is they are thinking about, what they may be afraid of. Sometimes writers write to solve a problem, to answer their own question. All these reasons are good reasons. And that is the most important thing I'll ever tell you. Maybe it is the most important thing you'll ever hear. Ever."

"Some writers write to earn money," said Evie.

"They do," said Ms. Mirabel. "But that is only one reason to write. And usually not the most important."

"What if we have nothing to write

about?" I asked. "And how do we change life by writing?" I added.

Miss Cash smiled.

"Lucy doesn't think her life is very interesting," she said.

My life *wasn't* interesting. Unless you counted my mother's cancer. Her cancer filled up the house these days. *Sadness* filled up my house. Sadness was all I knew. How could I change that?

"Well, she's wrong," said Ms. Mirabel. She walked over to stand in front of me.

"You have a story in there, Lucy," she said, touching my head. "Or a character, a place, a poem, a moment in time.

When you find it, you will write it. Word after word after word after word," she whispered.

The school bell rang. Ms. Mirabel jumped slightly. No one moved. Then, after a moment, Miss Cash took Ms. Mirabel's arm and they went out the door. We all picked up our notebooks and went off to try to change our lives. Word after word after word.

Chapter 2

We sat under Henry's huge lilac bush next to his house, the four of us: May and Henry, Evie and I. In a month or two, the smell of lilacs would fill the air.

"So, what do you think?" I asked.

No one said, "What do you think about *what*?" Everyone knew what I meant.

"I like her," said Evie. "Even if she sends her pathetic kids to camp all summer long."

"I think I love her," said Henry. "She tells the truth."

"Or maybe not. Maybe she lies," I pointed out.

"Right," said Hen, smiling. "Real and unreal are the same thing. So she says."

"What do you suppose that means?" asked May.

No one answered.

"Do you think she is happily married?" asked Evie thoughtfully. "She might be very good for my father."

"Evie, you can't just pick out some woman for your father," I said.

"Why not?" said Evie. She turned and looked at me, her face fierce. "Why not?"

Then her face crumpled and she began to cry.

I put my arms around her.

Henry's mother, Junie, put her iced tea glass on the windowsill and leaned out.

"Is everything all right out here?" she asked.

"Fine," said Henry.

Junie, who knew better but didn't say so, backed away through the window. Junie was the only mother we called by her first name because Henry did. And he called his father Max. Max worked at home because he loved Junie, and spent his time working on the computer and looking at Junie.

"They are like kids," said Hen once. "Sometimes I am the grown-up. I don't mind."

The steam from a pie on the table rose out the window. I watched a drop of water slip down the glass of iced tea as Evie cried on my shoulder.

After a while Evie stopped crying and leaned back. I could feel the sudden wet coolness the tears had left on the shoulder of my T-shirt.

"I'm a big, fat crybaby," said Evie loudly. "Big, fat crybaby."

"No," I said at the same time May did.

"You're not fat," said Henry.

Evie began to laugh then, and we all laughed, leaning back under the lilac bush, getting leaves and bits of dirt in our hair.

"Not fat at all," repeated Hen, making

us laugh harder. I could almost see the laughter as it rose up and wound around the branches of the lilac bush, touching the blooms before lifting up to the sky. I took out my notebook.

> *Sadness is*
> *Steam rising,*
> *Tears falling.*
> *A breath you take in*
> *But can't let out*
> *As hard as you try.*
>
> —Lucy

Chapter 3

The class was quiet—no coughing, no rustling of papers—at the sight of Ms. Mirabel. She wore a bright pink jacket trimmed with what looked like feathers. She wore long earrings that had feathers, too.

Maybe she would fly around the room, words falling like bird droppings on all of us.

"I am going to sit in the back today," said Miss Cash. "It will be Ms. Mirabel's class. Think of her as your teacher. She will be visiting us for six weeks, sometimes on a daily basis. At times she'll be in charge of the class. Sometimes I will be."

The windows were open, and the breezes rippled the feathers on Ms. Mirabel.

"I'm going to read some things to you," said Ms. Mirabel. "Words. Some

I hope you will like. You may not like some of what I read. You don't have to like everything."

We all looked at one another. Miss Cash had never told us we didn't have to like the things she read. I looked quickly at Miss Cash, but her face was still and stony.

"Some words may make you happy, some may make you sad. Maybe some will make you angry. What I hope"—a sudden gust of wind made Ms. Mirabel's hair lift—"what I hope is that something will whisper in your ear."

"What does that mean?" asked Russell.

Miss Cash sighed loud enough for me to hear. Russell always asked questions that made Miss Cash sigh.

Ms. Mirabel didn't sigh. She smiled brightly.

"You will know," she said.

Surprisingly, Russell grinned back at Ms. Mirabel as if they had a secret pact. Quietly, Miss Cash got up and opened the door at the back of the room and was gone.

Ms. Mirabel looked at us. "First, a place.

"The barn was very large. It was very old. It smelled of hay and it smelled of manure. It smelled of the perspiration of tired horses and the wonderful sweet breath of patient cows."

"Charlotte's Web," someone whispered excitedly.

"I knew that," said Russell.

"Now, a moment, a time, a place," said Ms. Mirabel.

"The road that led to Treegap had been trod out long before by a herd of cows who were, to say the least, relaxed. It wandered along in curves and easy angles, swayed

off and up in a pleasant tangent to the top of a small hill, ambled down again between fringes of bee-hung clover, and then cut sidewise across a meadow.

"Characters," said Ms. Mirabel. And she began to read.

"'Did Mama sing every day?' asked Caleb. 'Every-single-day?' He sat close to the fire, his chin in his hand. It was dusk, and the dogs lay beside him on the warm hearthstones.

"'Every-single-day,' I told him for the second time this week. For the twentieth

time this month. The hundredth time this
year? And the past few years?

"'And did Papa sing, too?'

"'Yes, Papa sang, too. Don't get so
close, Caleb. You'll heat up.'

"He pushed his chair back. It
made a hollow scraping sound on the
hearthstones, and the dogs stirred.
Lottie, small and black, wagged her tail
and lifted her head. Nick slept on.

"I turned the bread dough over and
over on the marble slab on the kitchen
table.

"'Well, Papa doesn't sing anymore,'
said Caleb very softly."

I smiled. I knew that story.

"Now a memory," said Ms. Mirabel.

"The memory is this: a blue blanket in a basket that pricks her bare legs, and the world turning over as she tumbles out. A flash of trees, sky, clouds, and the hard driveway of dirt and gravel. Then she is lifted up and up and held tight. Kind faces, she remembers, but that might be the later memory of her imagination. Still, when the memory comes, sometimes many times a night and in the day, the arms that hold her are always safe."

Ms. Mirabel smiled. "And a poem,"
she said.

> *"A nut*
>> *My poem.*
> *When cracked you'll find inside*
>> *Words*
>> *Whispers*
>> *People*
>> *Place*
> *That tuck in snugly to make*
>> *Story."*

Ms. Mirabel read on and on, some
things I'd heard before, some things I

hadn't. The breezes came in and around us like the words Ms. Mirabel spoke. No one moved, even when the bell rang for lunch.

Ms. Mirabel stopped.

"Maybe tomorrow some of you will bring your writing. You don't have to read it if you don't want to. I can read it for you. When we talk about it, we will be very kind. We will talk about what we like, and we will ask questions."

Ms. Mirabel waved her arm toward the door, her bird feathers rippling. "Go," she said.

And we went.

Hollow boned
Birds
Sing!
Until the sun falls down.
They tuck themselves under the
Green leaves of trees
And sleep until the sun calls
      them to
Sing again!

                                      —Henry

Chapter 4

We sat in Evie's bedroom, Evie hiding behind the curtain, looking across the yard to the house next door. A woman was moving things inside.

"A new neighbor. She looks healthy,"

said Evie. "She has short, curly, yellow hair. Actually, she's beautiful."

"Not that it matters," reminded Henry.

"Of course," said Evie. "My father doesn't need a beautiful woman. Just a woman."

May and I laughed.

Evie's cat, Looley, came in, saw us, and hissed before he began to frantically lick himself.

Evie's brother, Thomas, came, too, carrying two empty pots from the kitchen. He sat them down and began stirring each with a wooden spoon. The light came in the window and touched his blond hair. He was short and stocky like a rain boot.

"Hello, Thomas," said Henry. "What's up?"

"Soup," said Thomas seriously.

"Two pots of soup?" asked Henry.

Thomas nodded as he stirred.

"One is good. One is bad," said Thomas.

"Which is which?" I asked.

Thomas looked up and smiled.

"Guess."

We laughed. Evie smiled as her father came into the room to scoop up

Thomas. He leaned down to kiss Evie on the top of her head.

"We're going for a bike ride," he said.

"Look, Papa," said Evie. "An interesting woman is moving in next door."

Her father leaned next to her to peer out the window.

"Ah, yes," he said.

After they left, Evie smiled at us.

"He said 'ah'—did you hear?"

"Your father always says 'ah,' Evie," I said.

Outside, her father rode down the driveway, past our window, Thomas sitting on a seat behind him wearing a helmet.

"I don't have one thing in the world to write about," said May. "My life is the same, day in, day out."

"You're lucky," said Evie.

"You could make up something drastic," said Hen.

"Drastic?" said May. "Like what?"

Hen shrugged.

"Disaster. Violence. Alienation," said Henry promptly. "I read those words on the back of an adult novel the other day."

"I don't have any of that," said May.

"How about this," said Henry, frowning. "How about I push you. A little violence."

May laughed.

"Do you see any kid stuff? Bicycles, toys?" I asked Evie, knowing that is what she was looking for.

"Nothing!"

Evie came out from behind the curtain and looked at us.

"She's single," she announced matter-of-factly. "I know it!"

"Evie," said May, "what if your father doesn't want a new woman?"

May's voice was so quiet that we all

looked up. There was silence. Evie's face was still and thoughtful. Finally, she picked up her notebook. She opened it.

"I have a character anyway. Like Ms. Mirabel says."

She wrote something down.

I looked out the window and watched the woman next door carry a box into the house. A cloud passed over the sun, darkening the grass and trees for a moment.

"Her name is Sassy DeMello," said Evie.

"Sassy DeMello??!" hooted Henry.

"What kind of a name is Sassy?"

"Do you mean your character's name or the name of the woman next door?" I asked.

"Both," said Evie. "I like Sassy. She looks a bit like a Sassy."

We burst out laughing, but Evie ignored us. She put down her notebook and walked to the window to look out.

"What do you think?"

"I think you are a very funny girl," said Hen. "And probably you will be an amusing writer."

Evie turned to grin at Henry. She hadn't smiled much lately, and we

all smiled back at her. Then she got
serious. It was a little like the cloud
passing over the sun again.

"But Henry," she said. "This isn't
funny."

"I know," said Hen.

She has come here after a sad time. Sassy
has left much behind: her home, her life,
the friends who made her smile. The sun
lights up her loneliness. But she won't be
lonely for long. I will save her.

I will save my father, too.

—Evie

Chapter 5

The next day May came to school with a grim look, and Russell came with his writing.

"May? You look thunderous," said Henry.

"Hen, you've been reading the

dictionary," I said.

"I have."

"My very, very, very dumb mother is going to adopt a very, very dumb baby," said May.

"Too many *verys*," said Hen.

"There can never be too many *verys* about this," said May.

"Your mother is not dumb. She's smart," I said.

"Until now she was smart," said May.

"There's one thing," I said.

"What?" grumped May.

"You have something to write

about," I said. "And I sure wouldn't mind having a brother or sister."

"Get a cat," said May.

She glared at me and stomped to her seat.

Ms. Mirabel watched her. Ms. Mirabel wore purple today. Everything was purple: her skirt, her top, her shoes, her headband that failed at holding back that hair.

"Is there trouble?" she asked.

"A new baby at May's house," said Hen. "Her parents are adopting."

"Ah," said Ms. Mirabel.

I thought about Evie's father saying
"ah."

"Does May have any brothers and
sisters?"

"Four sisters. May is the youngest
one."

Ms. Mirabel smiled.

"I remember loathing my baby
brother."

"Like outlines," said Hen.

"Like outlines," she repeated.

"You probably love him now. Right?"
I said to her.

She looked at me as if surprised

51

at the question.

"Your brother," I repeated.

Ms. Mirabel sighed. "No, Lucy. He's not a very nice person, as it turns out."

Ms. Mirabel shook her head as if chasing away thoughts. She looked at the class, everyone sitting quietly now.

"Let's read!" she said. "Russell? Did someone whisper to you?"

Russell got up and stood at his desk. The paper shook a bit in his hand.

"Yes."

"And who whispered to you?"

"My dog," said Russell. "Just before he died."

I'll fly away
Above the big maple tree
Where I peed every day.

I'll fly away
Above the garden
Where I dug up carrots
And radishes
Where I rolled in something
Bad smelling.
I liked running with you

And chasing balls
And sleeping under your quilt.
But now
I'll fly away.

—Russell

Chapter 6

Russell ducked under Hen's big lilac bush. We were five today. It was late afternoon, and shadows fell across the yard.

Russell wore a pack.

"What is that?" asked May loudly.

Inside the pack was a baby.

"My brother, Oliver," said Russell. "You've seen him before."

"I don't like babies," said May.

Russell smiled. He took Oliver out of his pack and sat him on his lap. "You'll like Ollie," he said. "There is not one bad thing about him."

And as if Oliver had heard Russell, he smiled and pumped his arms up and down.

"I babysit for Ollie every day after school."

Hen reached out and took Oliver's hand.

"That's why you don't play soccer?"

Russell nodded.

Oliver grinned and then reached out to May. May drew back.

"He likes you," said Russell. "Here." He handed Oliver over to May, who held him away from her, as if he were a package of trash. But Oliver didn't care. He leaned closer and closer to May until his head lay on her shoulder. Slowly, May put her arms around him and closed her eyes.

"I think he's wet," she whispered finally.

"Of course he's wet," said Russell

cheerfully. "He's always wet. My babysitting time is over pretty soon. I'll take him home and change him."

May still held on to Oliver. She didn't open her eyes. And when she did, she whispered to Russell again.

"That was a beautiful poem about your dog, Russell."

Russell nodded and picked up Oliver. He ducked out from under the bush and put Oliver back in his pack.

"He was a good dog," he said softly.

"What was his name?" asked May.

"Everett," said Russell before he disappeared in the shadows.

There is a soft sweet smell here.
The smell of somewhere far away
I may have been one time but
can't remember.

It is a soft sweet smell.

Why is it I know it? Why is
it so familiar?

I can almost reach out my
hand to catch it.

But not quite.

—May

Chapter 7

My house was quiet. No music, no conversation, no laughing. I closed the door and walked down the hallway into the living room. My mother was staring at herself in the mirror. She did that a lot these days, since she had lost her hair from chemo. She saw me looking at her looking at herself.

"What do I look like, Lucy?" she asked me. "I look like *something*."

"An ostrich," I said.

Mama smiled.

"I do," she said.

She took a breath.

"What happened at school today? How is the beautiful and creative Ms. Mirabel?" she asked.

"She is beautiful and creative," I said.

"And how is that hair?"

"Robust," I said.

I smiled at her because she knew that was one of my vocabulary words.

Mama's hair was growing back, in small fuzz all over her head. She did look a bit like an ostrich. But she said she was getting better. *That's what she said. That's what mattered.*

"Russell wrote a poem about his dog dying," I said. "He brought his baby brother, Oliver, under the lilac bush."

"Russell?" asked Mama. "Russell who drives Miss Cash to distraction?"

"He drives her to sighs," I corrected her.

"Well, Ms. Mirabel seems to be

working miracles," said Mama. "What about you? Have you written anything for Ms. Mirabel?"

I shook my head, thinking about my poem about sadness. That's all I wrote about these days. *Sadness*.

"One poem. I'm waiting for something to whisper to me."

"Whisper? I am sure there are whispers all around you, Lucy."

Mama turned back to look in the mirror again.

"Maybe you aren't listening. Children hear everything. Children know everything."

Mama and I looked at each other in the mirror for a moment. Then the front door slammed shut.

"That's your dad," said Mama. "How can we convince him to take us out for dinner?"

"Tell him we're having liver."

Mama laughed. She didn't laugh much these days, and I liked the sound of it.

"Jack," she called as we hurried to the kitchen. "Lucy thinks I look like an ostrich!"

"I was thinking that very same thing,"

Papa called back. "What a smart girl she is!"

"And, Jack," added Mama. "We're having liver!"

"NO!" came a cry from the kitchen.

The moon came through my window. Soon it would begin to move away. I could hear my mother and father talking in the living room as if . . . as if nothing was wrong. I reached for my pad and pen. I would write something that would change life in my house. I would not write about sadness. Ms. Mirabel had said that she wrote to make life come out the way she wanted. Maybe I could do that, too.

MAMA

Sadness. Your laughter can't brush away the sadness here. I hear you trying to laugh. I see you trying to smile and trying to talk away the sickness.

You can't, you know.

You can't.

—Lucy

No use. It was still sadness. Sadness was all I had.

Chapter 8

We were under the lilac bush: Russell and Ollie, Henry, May, Evie, and I. Spring was turning into early summer. It was warm under the bush. Ollie was learning to crawl, and he pawed through the leaves and twigs beneath the bush. Russell watched him carefully so he wouldn't put sticks or stones in his mouth.

"He's getting around more now," said Russell. "Getting into my things sometimes. He likes my shoes."

"Like a puppy," I said.

Russell nodded.

"And soon words will float out of his mouth like clouds," he said. "Word after word after word, like Ms. Mirabel says."

"That sounds like a poem," I said to Russell.

"It does," agreed Russell. "I will

surprise you with it one day soon."

I smiled at him.

"My mother and father are getting ready to bring home their new baby," said May. "Theirs, not mine," she added.

Russell laughed.

"That is mean, you know," he said. "That baby is yours, too."

"I know it's mean," said May. "But I don't want that baby. I want Ollie."

Ollie crawled over to May in a lurching way and offered her a stick.

"Everybody wants Ollie," said Russell.

Inside the house we heard Junie

playing music. She began to sing, her sweet voice filling the air above us. We were quiet, listening. Ollie sat back on his haunches, looking up through the leaves of the lilac bush as if looking for the song.

When Junie stopped, Ollie made a chirping noise.

"He wants more," whispered Russell.

We were quiet, waiting.

"You know," I said, "I'm not sure Ms. Mirabel is right. She writes to try to change her life, but that doesn't work for me. Writing about my mother's sickness hasn't worked."

"Like my father needing a new wife," said Evie.

"And my mother's ugly baby to come," said May.

"My dog, Everett," said Russell. "I know that can't change."

I turned to Henry.

"But you don't write to change anything, Hen."

Henry shook his head as his mother began singing again.

"No," he whispered, so low we all leaned forward to hear him.

"I write to save everything I have," he whispered.

The song
The music
The words
Flow together
To make the things I have
Stronger.

—Henry

Chapter 9

M s. Mirabel came to class on Monday with a plastic bag filled with dirt. She took books and papers and a vase filled with flowers off the desk.

We watched as she lifted the bag

and poured the dirt all over the desk. I looked at Miss Cash at the back of the room. Her eyes were wide with surprise.

"This is important to writing," said Ms. Mirabel, ignoring our looks. "That is, it is important to my own writing. This . . ."—she paused—"is landscape! Mine.

"This dirt came from the prairie where I was a child. I played in it, dug in it, planted in it, and walked over it. It is where I began. And all my writing begins with a landscape such as this. A place."

"The lilac bush," said Hen out loud, making all of us smile.

"You have a landscape, do you?" said Ms. Mirabel.

"My tree house," said May.

"The field where the white cow lives," said Russell.

Ms. Mirabel smiled.

"You know, we don't always write about our landscape; but we have to understand how important place is in our poetry, our stories. Your character lives in a place that helps shape that character."

Suddenly, Ms. Mirabel looked

beyond us all, to the back of the room.

"Yes? Miss Cash?" said Ms. Mirabel.

"I have a jar of ocean water on my windowsill at home," said Miss Cash.

"Your place," said Ms. Mirabel softly. "You see? We all have a place where we begin. And I'll read you something I wrote about my place when I was your age."

"Our age?" asked Russell.

"Your age, Russell. I was your age once," said Ms. Mirabel flatly.

"The soft, silver feel of the dirt under my feet will always be there—in the wrinkles

*of my skin, in the beating of my heart. In
every single word I ever say."*

Ms. Mirabel stopped and looked
at us.

"You are a very good writer," said
Hen.

Ms. Mirabel smiled.

"You know what?" she said softly.
"So are you. So are *all* of you."

She took out a dustpan and brush
and began sweeping up the dirt and
putting it back in the bag.

Class was over.

We walked down the street without talking and along the park path on the way to Henry's house.

"Stop," said May suddenly. "Where's Ollie?"

Russell smiled.

"He has a doctor's appointment."

"Is he sick?" asked May, looking scared.

Russell shook his head and began walking again.

"A checkup. Maybe a shot."

May sighed.

"It isn't the same without Ollie."

"See," said Hen. "You like babies."

"I like *Ollie*," said May.

Russell laughed loudly and walked ahead, shaking his head. It reminded me of when Ms. Mirabel laughed about outlines.

We walked along the winding trail and came out at Hen's house. We crawled under the lilac bush. It was quiet again.

"It is funny to think of Ms. Mirabel at our age," I said.

Hen lifted his shoulders.

"She said we are good writers."

He looked at all of us.

"We are writers!"

Junie's music started from inside, and we leaned back against the woody branches of the lilac bush.

Henry grinned.

"Writers!" Henry repeated happily.

Except for me, I thought. *I'm not sure why I'm writing. My life is still about sadness.*

Chapter 10

Thomas sat in the midst of the buzzing and whirring of cars. Blue cars; green, red, white; one with flames painted on the sides. Some went by themselves, running on batteries; some were wound up by hand.

Late-afternoon light spread out across Evie's bedroom.

Thomas picked up the one with flames. "My favorite," he announced.

Hen held up the red car. "*My* favorite," he said.

"Mine's the blue," said May.

"Green," said Russell with feeling, making Thomas smile.

"She's coming for dinner," said Evie, rushing into her bedroom and leaning against the wall to catch her breath. We all looked at her. No talk, only the buzzing of cars.

"Sassy," said Evie. Her eyes gleamed.

She was excited.

"Sassy DeMello is coming for dinner?" asked Hen, smiling.

"Who is Sassy DeMello?" asked Russell.

"Evie's father's future wife," said May.

"Oh."

Evie couldn't speak. She nodded her head up and down.

"Who's cooking?" I asked. I had eaten Evie's food, and it was not delicious.

"My dad. He's making some mucky casserole."

"My mother loves mucky casseroles," said Hen. "She thinks they are French."

"Your mother is the most agreeable person I know," I said.

Hen smiled.

Evie's dad came into the room.

"Ah . . . ," he began, and we all burst out laughing at that.

"What's funny?" he asked, wiping his hands on a dish towel.

"I just baked a cake," he said. "How about that?"

"For Sassy?" asked Evie.

"Sassy?"

Evie's father looked mystified.

"Sassy from next door."

Evie's father started to laugh.

"Sassy? You mean Sister Mary Grace?"

"Sister?"

Hen started to smile but stopped because he saw Evie's face.

"Sister?" said Evie.

"You mean . . . ?" Evie began to speak, then stopped.

"Sister Mary Grace. She's a nun," said Evie's father. "She runs the preschool on Audubon Street. You'll like her," he added. An oven buzzer sounded in the kitchen. "And Mom's coming, too," he said as he hurried out.

Thomas looked up.

"Mama," he said in a small voice.

He looked at Evie, still standing against the wall.

"Mama?" he repeated.

Evie didn't speak. Slowly, she slid down to sit on the floor.

We all looked at one another, quiet, not knowing what to say.

A long time passed.

"You want to laugh," said Evie at last.

"Oh no," I said. "No."

"Yes," said Hen. "We do. And you will laugh, too."

Evie looked up.

"Nothing will make me laugh," she

said, her voice soft.

"Something will," said Hen.

"What?"

Hen smiled.

"Sister Sassy," he said.

It was quiet for a moment, then we began to laugh.

"Sister Sassy DeMello," said Hen.

And then it happened.

Evie laughed. And then, as if caught up by it, Thomas laughed, too, falling over into the colors of his cars.

Nothing is what you think.

A square is round

A circle is square

The earth is flat

The grass grows

Down,

The roots reach for

Sunlight,

Happy is sad.

And surprise!

When

Unhappiness comes

I smile.

—Evie

Chapter 11

"How was it?" I whispered to Evie.

"The dinner."

We stood outside the classroom.

"All right."

"Just a little all right? Or really all right?"

Evie looked up as if surprised at what she was about to say.

"Really all right. I told Sassy, I mean Sister Mary Grace, what I had named her. Sassy DeMello. She thought it was funny."

"It *is* funny."

"And Mama brought me a blank book for writing."

Evie took a deep breath.

"She said she wrote poetry and stories when she was my age. She kept them, and she'll show them to me if I want to see them."

Evie looked at me. And what she said was very sad.

"I never knew that about her," she whispered.

There wasn't anything to say. I knew about things that parents didn't tell you . . . that they were sick and maybe weren't getting better. They wrote poetry in books. They sang above the lilac bush. Who were they really? Parents thought you didn't know things, though my mama said children knew everything. What was unreal? What was real?

"I don't know," said Evie.

I realized I had said "What was real?" out loud.

I shook my head, suddenly feeling tears at the corners of my eyes.

"Mama moved back home again," said Evie. "Thomas is happy."

"And you?"

"I don't know," said Evie. She turned to look at me.

"Will I ever know what will last? What is real? Like you said?"

The school bell rang and we went inside, where in one of the mysteries and surprises of everyday life—something

that Sister Mary Grace Sassy DeMello
might call a miracle—Ms. Mirabel was
about to talk about real and unreal.

Ms. Mirabel was about to talk about
words.

Ms. Mirabel wore white today. White
skirt, white shirt, a white crocheted
headband trying to keep back her
hair. She moved around the room like
a cloud, pinning up our writing on
the walls around the room. Of course
there were her shoes: bright, startling
red. Magenta maybe?

"We have one more week," said

Ms. Mirabel. "Soon it will be summer and school will end. You have written poetry, many of you. And stories. And you have painted your own landscapes with stories. I'm leaving them up here so you can all read and reread them. And so your families can see them when they come for parents' night."

"So, what is next?" Russell blurted out.

Ms. Mirabel smiled.

"Real and unreal, truths and lies. Stories. And *words*," said Ms. Mirabel. She said *words* with the same hushed voice she had used the first day she came to class.

Beside me, Evie sucked in her breath.

"The first day you came you said real and unreal are the same," said Hen.

"I did," said Ms. Mirabel, smiling at him.

"How can that be?" asked Russell. "That doesn't make sense."

"Really?" said Ms. Mirabel slowly, as if she were about to catch Russell in a crab trap.

"Take Evie's poem—you don't mind

if we talk about your poem, do you, Evie?"

Evie shook her head with an alarmed look on her face. Ms. Mirabel walked over to the wall in her colorful shoes. She unpinned a paper.

"'Nothing is what you think,'" read Ms. Mirabel. "'A square is round; a circle is square. The earth is flat. The grass grows down, the roots reaching for sunlight.'"

She stopped and looked at Russell. "Do you think that is real? The grass grows down?"

"Well," said Russell, trying to figure out whether he should say yes or no. "No. The grass doesn't grow down."

"So, Evie is lying? Telling a non-truth?"

"No," said Henry. "We know what she means. She's using . . ." He paused. "She is using a figure of speech to make a point."

"Like what?" asked Ms. Mirabel.

"Well, a metaphor . . . the grass growing down is like everything not working right, working opposite than what she wants."

"And do you believe Evie in this poem?"

"Yes," said Russell and Hen and May at the same time.

"So she has used something unreal to say something real," said Ms. Mirabel. "*Metaphor*, good word. And have we learned what *simile* is?"

"Silly as slime," said Russell, nodding his head up and down. Everyone laughed.

"Sharp as a . . . ," said Ms. Mirabel.

"Cat's stare!" said Evie.

"Soft as . . ."

"The moonlight," said Hen.

Ms. Mirabel smiled at us.

"And what is the writer's tool in all of this? Making people laugh, or cry, or be angry, or think?"

The class was silent, staring at Ms. Mirabel.

She waited.

Henry's voice was soft in the room.

"Words," he said.

Ms. Mirabel looked as if she might cry. Her eyes gleamed.

"Yes," she said. "Magical words. Word after word . . ."

"After word," we all finished together.

She walked over to the wall and

pinned Evie's poem on the wall again. She turned.

"Go home," she said. "Go home and write me something about words."

Ms. Mirabel turned and walked out of the class. I looked back and saw Miss Cash smiling slightly, staring at the space that Ms. Mirabel had just left.

Chapter 12

The morning was bright; rays of light sloping across the room, the dust motes in them sparkling like gems. We were quieter than before, almost as if we were silently counting out the days left with Ms. Mirabel. Only two left.

Ms. Mirabel came in with Miss Cash, Ms. Mirabel in her feathered jacket and earrings. She knew we noticed.

"I'm running out of outfits," she told us. "It's almost time for me to go home."

No one spoke. Hen looked over at me and his eyes were sad, and I knew he thought of no more Ms. Mirabel, too.

Suddenly, the door opened and slammed shut, May leaning against it, out of breath. Her hair was rumpled, and her shirt was on inside out.

"May?" asked Ms. Mirabel. "Are you all right?"

May nodded.

"Baby's here. It's a boy. He's ugly, just like I thought."

Her words came in gasps. She looked at Russell and burst into tears.

Ms. Mirabel moved toward her, but Russell was faster. He put his arms around May, and she cried louder.

"You are crying because you are happy, not sad. Right?" he said.

May nodded.

"May, Ollie was so ugly when he was born that my mother said, 'Oh, poor little thing. I hope he pretties up soon.'"

May stopped crying and stepped

back and looked at Russell.

"His name is John Everett," she said.

Russell smiled at her. "Everett. My dog."

May nodded.

"My mother said I could pick the middle name."

"My dog," repeated Russell very softly.

"He's ugly," said May. She took a breath and blew it out. "But he's okay." She looked at us for a moment. Then she repeated, "He's okay."

It was quiet in the classroom then.

We all bent down to look at the empty
page of paper in front of us.

WORDS ARE

My mother's wordless humming

The smell of lilacs—

Sweet

Fragrant

Perfume

The sky

Looking up through branches:

Lace.

Old leaves,

Crumbling,

Old earth,
My home.

—Henry

BEAN BABY

There are no words for you,
little bean baby, little lima—
Boston baked—coffee bean.
You have no form. You have
no shape. There is no word for
you but one—
Love.

—May

"Wonderful writing. But here is one more." Ms. Mirabel picked up the paper and read:

> *"I am you*
> *And you are me.*
> *The only words that matter*
> *Are the words that say*
> *I am you*
> *And you are me.*
> *And we*
> *Are.*

"Is there someone here who wants to own this poem?" asked Ms. Mirabel.

It was quiet. Everyone looked around.

And then Miss Cash, at the back of the room, stood up.

"It is mine," she said shyly. She shrugged her shoulders. "Mine."

Chapter 13

It was the last hour of the last day of our last month with Ms. Mirabel. She wore a white blouse and blue pleated skirt and loafers. Not the kind of clothes she usually wore. She couldn't control her hair, however. It tumbled and surged over the collar of her blouse.

"This is what I used to wear when I was your age," she said. "I am one of you today. I am you and you are me, as Miss Cash wrote in her poem."

Miss Cash, at the back of the room, blushed.

Ms. Mirabel did look a little like us, except for the hair. There was no hair like Ms. Mirabel's hair.

She looked around at the walls where our writings hung.

"Your families are coming shortly to see what you've done."

"Ollie's coming," said Russell.

"And homely little John Everett," said May. "My mother and father don't like me to refer to him as ugly."

"Your parents will like your Baby Bean piece, May," Ms. Mirabel said.

"Sister Mary Grace is coming," Evie whispered.

"Sassy?" whispered Hen, grinning.

We laughed then, and Ms. Mirabel, who had no idea what we were whispering about, laughed with us anyway.

"I suspect," said Ms. Mirabel, "that your families will learn things about you they might not have known before when they read your writing. Perhaps they'll learn things about themselves, too."

She paused.

"Your writing is personal, and I hope you don't mind sharing it with your families."

"I mind a little," I said. "I wrote things that my mother has never heard from me before. I found out that it is me that changed with writing. Not my life."

"Yes," said Ms. Mirabel.

"And writing about my dog, Everett, made it easier for me to remember him," said Russell. "Kind of like you, Henry, writing things down to save them forever."

Ms. Mirabel smiled.

"You've all learned a lot about writing. And a lot about yourselves."

She turned to me.

"Do you want to take your poems down from the wall, Lucy? It is all right if you do," said Ms. Mirabel.

I thought about my mother, her hair growing out in longer spikes now. She looked more like a porcupine than an ostrich. But she was not pale anymore. And she was back to walking two miles a day.

I took a deep breath.

"No," I said. "I'm trying to be brave."

"Remember this if you remember anything from our time together," said Ms. Mirabel. "Writing . . . is . . . brave. You are brave."

We looked at one another nervously, trying to feel brave.

"I will miss you all," said Ms. Mirabel.

"We will miss you!" said Russell loudly.

We *would* miss her. What would we do without Ms. Mirabel? Would we write again? Would we ever talk again about things real and things unreal, things true and things that were lies? Would we ever be brave in our lives again?

It was like a daydream when our families came, bits of scenes and conversation drifting like smoke in a wind.

My mother cried when she read my poem about sadness.

"You never told me you were sad and scared," she said.

"You were sick," I told her.

"But you could have told me."

"No. It was too hard to say. But I could write it," I told her. "I finally wrote something that wasn't about sadness."

"Where is it?" asked Papa.

"Down there." I pointed to the far end of the bulletin board.

May's mother came with John Everett. Russell carried John Everett around and showed him people and desks and writing and Ms. Mirabel.

"How do you do, sweet thing?" said Ms. Mirabel. "You are beautiful. You don't look like a bean at all."

May's mother and father laughed.

"He was a bean at the beginning,"

she said. "May was right."

"She was," said May's father.

Hen's parents, Junie and Max, came, Junie wearing a colorful peasant skirt.

"I grew up in that house. I lived under that lilac just like Hen," said Junie when she read Hen's poem.

"You never told me that," said Hen.

"I guess I didn't think it was that important," said Junie.

"Everything is important," said Hen, sounding like an adult.

Junie burst into tears. Max grinned at Hen and put his arm around Junie. Was everyone going to cry?

"Ollie!"

Russell handed Bean Baby back to May and went to hold Ollie. Russell's mother was very quiet when she read Russell's poem about his dog. She was quiet for a long, long time.

"That is Everett's voice," she said at last.

"Don't cry," said Russell, alarmed.

"I won't promise," said his mother softly.

Sister Sassy, as Hen called her, and Evie's mother and father stood reading the poems. Thomas held Evie's hand.

"School," he whispered.

"I'm sorry," said Evie's mother. "I was thoughtless and selfish." She looked at Evie. "You are kind, and it is brave of you to write about saving your father."

"Evie," said Thomas to Ms. Mirabel.

"Yes," said Ms. Mirabel. "Your sister, Evie."

Thomas beamed at Ms. Mirabel.

"Evie is a good writer," said Ms. Mirabel.

"Evie," said Thomas.

"Evie."

"Evie."

Three times he said it to Ms. Mirabel,
like in a fairy tale.

Papa read my last poem to Mama. I
liked hearing his voice say my words. It
made the poem more real for me; more
important.

AWAY

Shut it away!

Sadness.

Lock the door after it!

Sadness.

Fold tears up and
Put them in a box
So they don't see
Light
Laughter
Joy!
Send sadness far away
So that even if you
Send for it
It doesn't hear you call.

—Lucy

It was warm under the lilac bush.
Russell was late. As always, Junie was
inside, humming something with no

words. The smell of baking came out the window above our heads.

"Cookies?" I asked.

"Pie," said Hen. "I bet on blueberry."

"How do you know that?" asked Evie.

"I know lots of things," said Hen.

"My mother cried," I said.

"Mine, too," said Hen.

"She sure did," said May.

Hen smiled.

We heard the sound of running, and Russell slid under the bush.

"Pie," he announced.

We laughed. Then it was quiet again.

"I wonder why it is the mothers who cry," said May.

"Fathers cry, too," said Evie. "I know that."

"Ollie said 'Mirabel,'" said Russell.

I smiled.

"He liked her," I said.

"Of course," said Hen in a soft voice.

"If this were a book," I said, "it wouldn't have an ending."

Hen turned to stare at me.

"Maybe the ending is that it doesn't end," he said.

"It goes on," said Russell cheerfully.

"Thank you, Ms. Mirabel."

Junie leaned out the window.

"Pie, lambs?" she called.

"What kind?" asked Hen.

"Blueberry!" said Junie.

Hen grinned.

"It goes on," he said.

He raised his hand. I tapped it.

"It goes on," I said.

Out of our writer mouths
Will come clouds
Rising to the sky
Dropping rain words below.

And when the clouds leave

The sun will shine down word

After word

After word

Planting our stories in the earth.

—Russell

Author's Note

Years ago I was asked if I would write a book about writing and what it was like to be a writer. When I sat down to write the book, I realized that this was a topic I talked about all the time with children, answering their questions in letters and visiting them in classrooms. I didn't want to go over the same stories of my life—where stories came from; where they started, how they changed; how I felt when writing was too hard and I got stuck; how I felt when my writing worked!

Instead of writing a nonfiction book I decided to write *Word After Word After Word*, the story of a well-known writer who visits a fourth-grade classroom.

I am certainly in this book. I can see myself as a child writer, trying to figure out what I had to say. And I can see myself as Ms. Mirabel, with her bag of dirt carried in a plastic bag. I have several of these bags in my house, next to my bed, in my pocketbook, and next to my computer, reminding myself of where I began as a child and the stories I brought with me.

Sometimes a fiction story has "truths" for the writer as well as the reader. I enjoyed getting to know the children in this book, and both Ms. Mirabel and Ms. Cash. They all now feel like family to me.

—*Patricia MacLachlan*

6/24/10